GOING UP!

Written by Sherry J. Lee   Illustrated by Charlene Chua

KIDS CAN PRESS

Today, Dad and I are invited to a party
on the tenth floor.

FROM: Francesca Pianalto

TO: Leonard and Sophie

You are invited to
Olive's birthday party.

WHERE: 10th floor party room

WHEN: Saturday from
2:00 to 4:00 p.m.

Dad and I baked our favorite cookies this morning to take to the party — molasses with jam in the middle, like a sandwich. It's my grandma's recipe. We put them on a special plate.

Dad holds the plate for me so I can push the button.

Going up!

The elevator stops on the second floor.

When the doors open, the Santucci brothers,
Andrew and Pippo, are waiting to get on.
    "Hey, Little Bit!"
    Pippo always calls me Little Bit.

Going up!

The elevator stops again on the third floor.
It's Vicky, Babs and their dog, Norman.

"Norman! I love you, too," I say, laughing.

Going up!

On the fourth floor, the elevator stops again and this time it's Mr. and Mrs. Habib from 407 with their grandkids, Yasmin and Jamal. They are holding a big bowl of gulab jamun.

"We made your favorite, you two,"
says Mrs. Habib.

Dad and I grin at each other and high five.

Just as
the door is
closing ...

"Wait for me!"

"Oh, hi, Mr. Kwan! Come on in!" Andrew says, holding the door open for him.

Going up!

The whole Flores family gets in on the
fifth floor, Miguel, Ana, Samuel, Raul,
Cleopatra and Baby Jade.

"Hey, guys!" says Raul. "We have our
dancing shoes on!"

"Hmm. Should I put you
on my shoulders so there's
more room, Soph?" asks Dad.

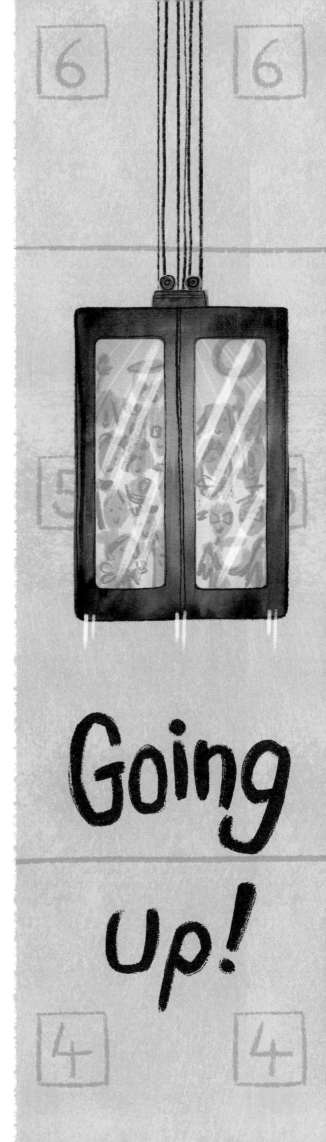

Going
Up!

When the elevator stops on the sixth
floor, it's Vi Tweedle and her Chihuahua,
Minx. Minx is carrying her yellow ball
in her mouth. She never goes anywhere
without her yellow ball.

"Lovely to see you, Vi," says Miguel.
"You are a picture!"

No one gets in on the seventh floor.

On the eighth, we have to hold the elevator while Grace and Arnie get in with their instruments: a clarinet and a bass. Arnie is wearing his sparkly glasses and porkpie hat.

"Yikes," says Vi. "Can we all fit?"

They squeeze in.
Everyone is giggling.

Going up!

The elevator stops on the ninth floor.

"Uh-oh," I say.
"Everyone take a deep breath in!"
says Mrs. Habib.

It's Nori!
"Squeeze in, Nori," says Vicky.

The elevator stops on
the tenth floor.

DI

"Happy birthday,

Going up!

Olive!"

The doors open.

For Kevin Joseph Harper, with gratitude — S.L.

To everyone who lived in Blk. 135 Bedok North St. 2, including Orange, the elevator cat — C.C.

Text © 2020 Sherry J. Lee
Illustrations © 2020 Charlene Chua

Kids Can Press gratefully acknowledges the financial support of the Government of Ontario, through Ontario Creates; the Ontario Arts Council; the Canada Council for the Arts; and the Government of Canada for our publishing activity.

Published in Canada and the U.S. by Kids Can Press Ltd.
25 Dockside Drive, Toronto, ON M5A 0B5

Kids Can Press is a Corus Entertainment Inc. company

www.kidscanpress.com

The artwork in this book was rendered in watercolor, watercolor ink and colored pencil, then scanned and digitally manipulated in Photoshop.
The text is set in Minya Nouvelle.

Edited by Yasemin Uçar
Designed by Michael Reis

Printed and bound in Malaysia, in 10/2019 by
Tien Wah Press (Pte) Ltd

CM 20 0 9 8 7 6 5 4 3 2 1

FSC
www.fsc.org
MIX
Paper from
responsible sources
FSC® C012700

Library and Archives Canada Cataloguing in Publication

Title: Going up! / written by Sherry J. Lee ;
illustrated by Charlene Chua.
Names: Lee, Sherry J., author. | Chua, Charlene, illustrator.
Identifiers: Canadiana 20190093897 |
ISBN 9781525301131 (hardcover)
Classification: LCC PS8623.E44375
G65 2020 | DDC jC813/.6—dc23